SHE'S FLEEING A BYRONIC HERO

SHE'S FLEEING A BYRONIC HERO

A ROMANTIC ROMP

LADY ALANA SMITHEE

EDITED BY
LADY LILITH SAINTCROW

SAINTCROW

For Her Ladyship Skyla, who hopefully finds this an acceptable offering...

I

THE CHASE BEGINS

Titness Agatha McHawttie, young and impecunious heir of Velvette, galloped across the vapor-swirling Heathencliffe Moors upon her faithful pink almost-unicorn Chicken, searching for escape. Behind her, the hounds of Byron, Lord Chestthumper, bayed and gamboled through the indirect moonlight.

Lord Chestthumper, who had fought more than one duel with persons who mispronounced his title, was a cad, if not a complete *rogue*; Titness could not believe she had been sold in marriage to such a fellow. But the pussies of her ancestral northern manor Velvette needed aid—and, truth be told, a vast quantity of delicate food fit for their noble stomachs—so she had agreed to the match in the interests of both feeding said felines, well represented upon the McHawttie family crest, and in repairing her crumbling—though very noble and ancient, indeed—ancestral manse.

She had, in fact, agreed well before she discovered

her very well-off intended was not the old, sickly man she had been led to believe.

No, Byron Blackheart was young, fit, likely to survive many years even if Titness poisoned him daily with philtres purchased on the sly from genuine certified beldams, and he had extremely large hands to boot. To make matters worse, Byron Blackheart was that most unrepentant of scoundrels, giving his affection to slavering, ill-bred creatures indeed.

He was, in short a *dog person*. The hounds of Chestthumper even slept in his lordly bedchamber, a thought which made the young Lady Velvette almost faint with rage, though truth be told the canines were quite winning creatures, soft-eyed and cold-nosed, and not nearly as prone to clawing and biting as the wild pussies of Velvette.

Nevertheless, a McHawttie was a Cat Person, and Blackheart was a Dog Person, and as far as Titness was concerned there was no chance of ruth *or* a joining of forces, even in holy matrimony. Despite that, her father's ire and Velvette's need of hard cash had pushed Titness to the altar that very morning. Indeed once the banns had been published she had no recourse at all, despite racking her quite adequate though hardly overabundant brains.

Her attempts at escape had been met with utter mischance, not to mention stony resistance—and once, a week ago in fact, Chicken's outright refusal to leave Velvette's warm, safe stable—and so Titness had been ignominiously wed to the man she had every reason to heartily dislike despite his rather brooding handsomeness.

Indeed, after a final pre-wedding night spent tossing and turning attempting to reason out a means of escape, while old Nursie slept upon the trundle and her father stood guard outside her door to prevent any escape unless through a tower window, Titness had been almost too exhausted to see the groom through her veil, and had yawned more than once in reply to the surpliced priest's exhortations to love, honour, and mumble-mumble whatnot.

Now, after one short day of marriage though still with her maidenly modesty quite intact, Titness—having been caught pouring a phial of suspect liquid into Blackheart's afternoon tea, not to mention spitting upon his crumpets—was fleeing for her life.

And her quasi-virginity, for she did not wish to lose Chicken.

Now, Titness had attended a quite aristocratic finishing school in Lowe Crampton with many other a highborn maiden, so she was perhaps in technical point of absolute fact not wholly and entirely a virgin, but it was good enough to keep her in an almost-unicorn's saddle. Besides, the thought of Lord Chestthumper's positively enormous hands upon her person caused such upheaval in Titness's ample and bouncing bosom she was, not to put too fine a point upon it, warmly bothered despite the thick, almost rancid evening fog.

So the young Lady of Velvette—now legally Mrs Blackheart—fled, giving little thought to such niceties as

food or a purse to pay for lodging since everyone knew
ladies have small appetites. Or so all the books and
governesses averred, though Titness was ravenous, and
even Chicken's pinkish haunches were beginning to look
rather enticing. The stuffed horn attached to a leather
strap crossing the mare's brow quivered like a custard,
and Titness began to wish she had at least filched a slice
of wedding cake or a spit-free crumpet at tea.

On through the night Titness galloped upon Chicken,
who thought the whole thing rather an affront since she
had been enticed from the Pemberwheeze estate's warm
stable with an apple slice, then made to prance across
the moors while dogs yipped and yapped behind her.
Consequently, the pink almost-unicorn—much better at
finding her way than Titness, who could frankly become
lost inside a burlap bag—galloped in circles as the moon
glowered upon the chase.

2

ACCEPTABLE SHORTCOMINGS

No one could ever call raven-haired Byron Perssy Blackheart lacking in courage, though more than three souls including his sainted late mother had privately thought him somewhat shy in the department of wit. At the moment, riding across the fogbound Heathencliffe Moors in the dead of night upon a black charger named Pickles, he was cold, damp, furious, and—truth be told —somewhat charmed.

It wasn't easy for a man with several estates including palatial Pemberwheeze, not to mention very large hands, to fend off matrimonial alliances; yet the instant he saw the McHawttie girl across a crowded ball-room he had changed his mind—a rather stunning occasion for one of his temper, indeed.

Once set, a lord of Chestthumper rarely wavered in his course.

Now he almost wished he had made an offer for his charming neighbour Hymenia Galore, Baroness Frostcunny instead, despite her oft-avowed and perhaps not quite jesting plan of sending every child in her ideal husband's very fine mansion to a very cold, very thrifty boarding school—except the peasants, of course, who could be put to work as soon as they could walk. Hymenia had a fine seat when she rode to hunt and the rest of her was tall, blonde, and quite imperious; not to mention she and Byron had been promised to each other from the cradle as far as the Galore aunt de Bourguignon was concerned.

If he were to tell the absolute truth, Byron was more than a little relieved Auntie de Bourguignon was buried in the churchyard he had ridden past just that afternoon, bringing his new bride home.

The red-haired McHawttie had seemed a little more tractable than any other choice, hailing as she did from a highly noble though thoroughly penniless northern family, and besides, she had made quite agreeable conversation upon the subject of wine while her thoroughly distracting bosom pressed enticingly against her dress. In fact, since the moment he had seen the young lady Byron had not quite been himself, and sworn inwardly that he would have no other girl for his bride.

Unfortunately, the lord of Pemberwheeze Chase was heartily regretting his choice as Pickles—the black charger was named thus for his regrettable fondness for fermented vegetables, a trait passing strange in a horse —galloped in pursuit of a pinkish-white mare bearing a short, plush, curved horn strapped to her forehead.

The prematurely aged Lord Velvette had explained

that Titness—for that was the name of Byron's new bride, a name he had not managed to pronounce more than once or twice from the moment he saw her until this very day—hotly and continually averred the pinkish creature a unicorn disfigured by tragic childhood accident, and her parents had allowed the misapprehension to continue in the interests of keeping the girl's Reputation spotless before her eventual and hopefully advantageous Marriage. At the time Lord Chestthumper had thought it a fine solution, and if it bespoke a certain lack of Reason in his new bride, surely such a shortcoming was quite acceptable in a wife, for after all dogs were fine creatures unburdened by much in the way of Logic but full of Obedience.

His new bride had promptly adulterated his tea with something from a small patent-medicine phial and also spat quite accurately upon his crumpets, showing a high degree of spirit and even better aim. Byron might even have complimented her upon the latter, for he knew from experience how difficult proper expectoration could be. Unfortunately, upon being caught in the midst of that operation, she had fled through the very large Chestthumper mansion with a scream quite unbecomingly like a tea-kettle's—and all this despite his loud and vociferous attempts to reassure her that he bore no ill will at all!

Byron had thought it best to let the lady's nerves settle a bit, especially since he was somewhat nervous about the performance of connubial duties. Yet when dinnertime came, his new wife was nowhere to be found and the pinkish mare was missing from the warm, exceedingly comfortable Pemberwheeze stable.

Byron believed animals, being of far more use and genuine good nature than most people, deserved snug rest. Pickle concurred, and indeed, was known to kick his stall to pieces should accommodations not measure to his standard.

The lord of Chestthumper had even thought his new bride was of like temper, for she spoke charmingly of the pussies of her home, visibly treasured her mare, and was most solicitous of the pinkish beast's comfort. Byron had been looking forward to some version of marital harmony and perhaps a wife who did not mind his lack of experience in...certain areas, being virginal herself.

Now he was roundly disabused of the notion, and had missed dinner to boot.

Perhaps that was why his vision wavered, and as Pickle sailed over a half-seen obstacle—probably the broken-down gate near the millpond, though they seemed to have passed it already twice upon this most vexing evening—it might have been hunger which caused Byron Blackheart's very capable hands to weaken slightly upon the reins. The hounds yapped and bayed most excitedly, though no few of them were missing their own suppers and wished to draw this enjoyable jaunt to its natural conclusion in order to remedy that lack.

In any case, there was a great jolt, Pickle snorted as he landed, the hounds were busy discussing the day's many upsets and changes amongst themselves, and neither charger nor canines quite noticed that their master had left them.

In fact, Lord Chestthumper landed with a quite unbecoming "*Oof,*" upon the far side of the gate near the Snivvelings mill-pond, and lay stunned for quite some time, listening to hoofbeats and barking recede in the distance.

Left to his own devices, large, glossy, practical Pickle —now free of his lordly burthen—decided to turn for home upon his own recognizance since they had been going in circles for a good two hours anyway.

3

DEWBADDE'S QUANDARY

DUDLEY DEWBADDE, FOR THREE WEEKS A FULLY VESTED highwayman with the Sneak and Vicious Collective, would *normally* not have hailed the redhead upon the pink pony as she galloped past.

He only did so because it was a very dark and foggy evening in this section of Wystywych Lane, and indeed, upon the village, mill, palatial manor, and outlying estates clinging to the edges of Heathencliffe Moors, and consequently he did not notice her hair until it was too late.

Despite bearing a brace of pistols, a very large curved knife, and a terribly aesthetic but not quite serviceable dagger tucked in his knee-high black leather boot, Dudley made a point of never trucking with gingers since he had once passed words with a wandering beldam in his youth.

The raddled dame, possessed of a glass eye and a quite fetching smile missing one of its canines under a mass of heavily powdered wig-curls suspiciously like horsehair, had first informed young Duds that he was the illegitimate son of a great man—which was true enough, though Dudley's mother had sworn the boy to secrecy upon that point and until then, young Duds had considered it a possible, though affectionate, maternal falsehood—but then followed by informing the lad that if he ever attempted to prick a redhead, his codger would fall free and run away.

Of course it was ridiculous and the beldam had no doubt merely taken a drop too much gin, but Dudley had not achieved his position in the Sneak and Vicious Collective by being incautious. Wystywych, despite its name, was rather a plum of an assignment, and Duds had ensured he was voted to cover it by dint of cunning, unbending stubbornness, and the quite respectable practice of outright buying support among one or two of his brethren.

If 'twere good enough for Parliament, Dudley thought, bribery was quite acceptable for a man attempting to support his elderly and quite thrifty mum with a bit of highway robbery.

But it was still a deeply fogbound and very dark evening despite the moon, and very cold besides. To add to his startlement, one simply did not see a small pinkish mare with some strange appliance strapped to its forehead every day—or night. So it was that Dudley heard the approaching hoofbeats and sprung from the shrubbery with his usual aplomb, plus a shouted, *"Stand and deliver, I say,"* in quite the usual and accepted way.

The horse reared, there was a feminine expostulation which bordered upon the shrill, and when the surprised, plump, pinkish beast galloped off, what remained was the crumpled form of a young lady with disheveled hair very *definitely* of the ginger persuasion, a very fine purple cloak, and under said cloak a tea-gown of beautiful Bridgerton blue which would fetch a pretty penny even with a stain or two. Her boots were dainty, her bosom was exceedingly capacious, and she was understandably knocked senseless.

Dudley, a rather strapping black-haired young man, stood for a few moments near the handy shrubbery lining this portion of Wystywych, allowing himself some thought. It was not an operation he engaged upon often outdoors, having very little need of deep reflection during the endless and often rain-drenched waiting to halt coaches full of terrified respectables, squeeze off a pistol shot, and collect their valuables.

Not that anyone in the Collective was called upon to perform such an operation with any regularity, Snivvelings Village being what it was. Petty egg-theft from local coops and bouts of fisticuffs in the small, also local tavern were the more usual occupations for Duds and his friends; the strapping young lad was much more used to cogitating upon the proper price for articles filched from said tavern's lost-and-found, or brushing up his next speech for the Collective's interminable meetings than anything else.

Obviously he could not leave the girl in the lane; it promised, after all, to be a very damp night. Dudley nervously stroked the tips of his very fine dark moustache, conscious that his bottle-green velvet jacket was hardly thick enough for the weather. Still, it looked very dashing, and a highwayman, *especially* of the Collective, had a certain standard to uphold. One could simply never tell when a toothsome dame with a weakness for dashing rogues might appear, or a pose might need to be struck while escaping an officer of the King's Law, especially if said escape involved swinging upon a rope over the Big Dippling Gorge in the next county, as the leader of the Collective was rumored to have done.

But if Duds left his post, a fat carriage stuffed with jewel-dripping respectables might come along. The fact that one never had before was of little import, since the Collective decreed Wystywych was the most likely place for an inaugural event of that type and Dudley had, against all odds, secured this appointment by hook and crook.

He quite intended to be the first to perform such a feat. With most of the other honourable members of Sneak and Vicious engaged upon the far more laborious but undeniably more profitable acts of local thuggery or small home repair bringing some coin into the Collective's coffers, the Wystywych post was also the job requiring the finest clothes—borrowed from the Collective's collective closet—and least amount of effort, two things which suited Widow Dewbadde's loving son perfectly.

Having thoroughly ruminated upon his quandary while an owl hooted in nearby Lanolin Woods—more properly a thicket, and bordering upon the Snivvelings mill-pond between the shed and the mill itself on the village side—Dudley decided there was nothing for it. He would have to carry the unconscious, top-heavy, dangerous redhead to said nearby shack sometimes used for the drying and storage of fish from the mill-creek, secure her for the time being in the one battered chair the shack somehow still retained, visit his mother for some good advice upon this development, and return forthwith to his post. Once his shift upon the Lane was done, he could also consult the Collective and some form or another of ransom might lift their small enterprise to a slightly higher level of malfeasance, theft, and perhaps even revolution?

Of course, Dudley thought revolution sounded a bad idea, leading as it did to stomach upset and dizziness, but as their leader had pointed out, one couldn't have a Collective without a Higher Goal, and Thomas Sawyere —for that was the name of the Collective's head—was never a lad to think small.

Only one vexing question remained—how would young Dewbadde remove the girl to the fish-shed without touching her? Duds didn't *truly* think his trouser-snake would go walkabout if he laid a fingertip upon a redheaded miss, but there was, as his mother often said, no use in tempting fate.

The widow usually delivered this piece of advice while staring balefully into the fire after a drop or two of bitter, and that was inevitably the point at which Dudley stopped listening, for the story of her seduction by a careless rake who only paid a few pounds per annum to support little Duds would come next. Those pounds managed to keep Widow Dewbadde—the village, of course, all affected to believe her fictitious husband dead in the quite real Peninsular Wars—in something approaching comfort or at least lifted above absolute penury, and able to supplement it with a thriving trade in potions and simples besides.

Either way, Dudley rather liked his anatomy in the shape it currently held, and did not long after any subtractions. And when he heard the approaching gallop of a single horse and a great baying of hounds, he was seized by the sudden certainty that it would be very advisable indeed to quit Wystywych Lane for a short while despite being on duty, not to mention give a quick visit to his mum to make sure she was doing all right, and besides he could not very well leave a bosom so bounteous to be trampled by dogs, even if it *was* attached to a redhead.

In a trice he had leapt to the poor somnolent thing's side, bent to grasp her cloak with his gloved hands—the glove-leather was very slippery, it being a very damp night indeed—and proceeded to haul Titness McHawt-tie, now Titness Blackheart, into the thorn-laden shrubbery.

4

THE BARONESS'S RAMBLE

HYMENIA GALORE HAD NOT STARTED THE DAY INTENDING TO lodge in a flea-bitten inn, but what else could a scorned baroness do in this situation? Bad enough the exceedingly silly—though admittedly, reasonably handsome—Lord Chestthumper had not yet made an offer of alliance to the great neighbouring house of Frostcunny, but such a thing could be borne temporarily so long as the eventual end was assured.

So Baroness Frostcunny had waited, visited Pemberwheeze Chase near-weekly upon one pretext or another, petted silly Byron's dogs—they were quite noble animals, really, despite the smell when they were fed something disagreeable—and bided her time, knowing she was the most attractive, not to mention richest lass from here to London, which was saying something indeed.

To have such a highborn and remunerative Galore spurned in favor of an almost Gretna Green-quick marriage to a penniless, though aristocratic enough, redheaded northern tart was consequently *quite* a vexation. Why, if Hyemnia's old aunt de Bourguignon was alive, she would be howling about the pollution of the shades of Pemberwheeze before dramatically fainting, requiring smelling salts and a large application of sherry to settle her nerves.

Of course dear old Auntie had many a time impressed upon young Hymenia the need to reacquire the ancient missing half of Frostcunny's estates by an advantageous marriage with the Chestthumper heir, even if said heir barely noticed Hymenia's existence since she did not have soft flopping ears, a fur coat, and a wagging tail. Still, it should not have been any great difficulty for a young lady of consequence, means, blonde curls, and a most fetching instep.

But the little McHawttie coquette had scooped up Byron Blackheart's estate and several thousand pounds a year, as well as the title *Mistress of Pemberwheeze Chase*, so Hymenia was forced to alternative measures. Which meant not only had she lodged in a verminous inn under an assumed name, with a heavy veil to keep her Reputation intact and Identity secret, but those considerations had also forced her to skirt the village fringes instead of walking through its very center. Consequently, she was now wandering on foot in the dark of a foggy autumnal night, looking for a certain ill-repaired shack upon the far edge of Snivvelings Village, right where said tiny townlet petered out into Heathencliffe Moors.

In that tiny thatched domicile was a witchlike crone

Hymenia's old Nursie swore could mix a potion of illicit nature and deeply unreligious effects, suitable for ensnaring a somewhat foolish—even if reasonably handsome and quite well financially endowed—male. Once administered, the philtre should solve a certain baroness's current quandary. The fact that it would require throwing over a penniless though aristocratic northern hussy, possibly ruining the McHawttie girl's Reputation and consequently her chances of another advantageous match, was merely the way the biscuit crumbled.

Yet it was dreadfully cold, hideously damp, very dark, and while Hymenia had ridden through Snivvelings several times in a carriage or upon a fine blooded mare during annual hunts, she had never walked.

As a result, the young Baroness Frostcunny was completely, irredeemably, and absolutely lost.

Consequently, when she saw a glimmer of water in the darkness, she was extremely displeased and almost muttered a very improper word or two. The mellifluous glitter could have been the ancient Butock River for all she knew, which would mean she had walked for miles —a feat not entirely beyond her powers but quite unladylike, and especially vexing upon this particular evening.

"Oh, *bother*," Hymenia muttered, and just as she was about to whisper another—and much more unladylike —word, her foot encountered something soft, and she realized the watery gleam was a mill-pond.

In fact, it was far side of the mill-pond near Pemberwheeze Chase, not the Wystywych side, which meant her destination was relatively near after all, and her relief was almost as considerable as her very fine— though not quite as capacious as a certain McHawttie's —bosom. However, she stubbed her toe *again* upon that soft, oddly firm thing, and a low, distinct groan reached her ears.

For a moment the young baroness contemplated the advisability of fleeing into the night, possibly with a maidenly scream, but the distant, flickering golden gleam of a candle behind the scraped horn window of what should be a rundown though very picturesque shack was temptingly within reach. And, as she hesitated, the corpse at her feet—for she had decided this was a recently murdered body, just as in the last scandalously good novel she read—gave yet another shapeless moan, and she recognized the voice.

Instead of spending his nuptial evening with his russet tartlet of a new bride, Lord Chestthumper had been cast literally at a baroness's dainty toes. Which was, Hymenia thought, rather a lovely turn of events, and showed that her plan was smiled upon by whatever powers were responsible for looking after hard-hearted gentleladies.

Well, Hymenia's heart was not precisely flinty, though her beloved aunt de Bourguignon had done her best to make it so. The young Galore simply felt the entire burden of Frostcunny upon her shapely shoulders, and was determined to do her ancestors proud by making whole the family estate, sadly halved three hundred years ago by a certain syphilitic king during a fit of pique.

Perhaps it was the ancestors of Frostcunny who had placed Byron Blackheart upon her path. In any case, Hymenia bent, and found the silly man's arm by dint of feeling around, deciding a certain trunklike appendage was a leg and another something she should not be touching until she had poured the proposed potion down the man's throat, and finally striking her goal upon the third attempt.

"Up with you, dearest Byron," she cooed. "Come, let's go to the lovely little witch's house, shall we? A midnight walk, then a wee drink, and you'll be *quite* yourself again."

And she would be the mistress of Pemberwheeze Chase.

The night, as her aunt de Bourguignon might have remarked, was looking up.

5
ROPES AND KNOCKS

Regaining consciousness tied to a chair had certainly not been in Titness's plans. Of course, *"plan"* was a very loose descriptive term for what was going on inside her head as she attempted to poison tea, spat upon crumpets, and fled her new husband.

At first she was afraid she had been struck by some manner of religious punishment for her recent actions, as old Nursie—and several governesses—had more than once threatened the young Miss McHawttie with. Titness was of the quite reasonable, though perhaps agnostic, opinion that the good Lord had better things to do than attend to her small mischiefs, since a young lady of high birth was often held by both Serious Academical Men and Satirists to be useless if unmarried and only marginally useful otherwise and such creatures were far below the notice of any Almighty worth the name.

But as Titness blinked, peering through disheveled coppery curls falling into her quite conventionally attractive face, the stygian darkness she was trapped in took on some edges and gleams of colour, and she realized she was in a small wooden-walled space which qualified as a shack. There was a rather strong odor of rot, another of damp, and the bonds about her were not nearly as tight as a corset but still quite uncomfortable.

"H-Hullo?" Titness whispered. It was perhaps not the best idea, since whoever had presumably tied her up might hear and return to wreak some damage upon her tender, helpless person. On the other hand, the malefactor had not gagged her, and her feet were free. She could kick, if she had to—though a young lady of her oft-undervalued intellectual stature could tell it might not do much good. "Oh, *bother*."

Slowly, as her poor straining eyes adapted to the gloom, she found she was not crowded by monsters or ruffians intent upon stealing her Virtue. That last point was hardly a comfort as she was now a married woman, but the thorny question of whether or not she counted as such since said marriage had not been consummated was for people with far more leisure than she currently possessed to argue over.

Titness took a deep breath. She was rewarded by a creaking in the rope wrapped sloppily about her torso, pinning her arms and securing her to what felt like a solid wooden kitchen chair. Her bosom strained as her lungs inflated, and the chair gave a short, unhappy groan.

Heartened by that slight sound, the new bride gave a serpentine hip-wiggle, much as girls at finishing school learned to do when seating themselves upon a crowded mealtime bench or practicing the many fine arts of Husband Hunting under the watchful gazes of spinsters —said arts proving useless in Titness's case, since she had done positively nothing to attract Lord Chest-thumper's attention except stare daggers at him after he stepped upon her toe during a waltz and make quite conventional conversation laced with every attempt to fend off his clumsy advances.

The chair creaked again.

"Kippers and milk," she whispered, a term of surpassing wonder featuring the two things the soft, warm pussies of her beloved Velvette loved best.

Then she took another whopping inhale, her fine and generous bosom pressing against sadly strained rope. Her pulse beat thinly in her ears, her lips skinned back from her pearly, dainty teeth, and when she could fill her lungs no further she let all the air out in a high, screaming whistle very much like a tea-kettle left too long upon the hob or a newfangled steam engine just before a truly regrettable explosion providing casualties fit to make the evening broadsheets.

Said whistle shivered against the walls of the battered fish-shack and floated free into the night. It was followed at a short interval by another, and another.

Titness held grimly to her new task, and was rewarded upon the fifth inhale by a popping, a snapping, and a whipcrack as the overstrained and now quite broken rope exploded from her throbbing torso. The chair shattered, and she was dumped quite inelegantly upon her backside.

Still, even a pratfall was cause for celebration in the current circumstances. Her bosom might have been a torment to her upper back and a distinct impediment to fleeing on foot, but it was also *extremely* useful for hiding small articles—or escaping the predicament as she currently found herself in. Her last whistle was louder than all the rest, for now she was free of all constraint, though supine amid the wrack and ruin of a distinctly plebeian chair.

After rubbing some semblance of life back into her arms and legs, young Mrs Blackheart, the new Lady Chestthumper, decided to explore her surroundings.

That was when she discovered she was indeed in a tiny fish-shack very near a body of water, and the door appeared to be locked—alas, from the *outside*.

A LESSER MAN than Byron Blackheart might have remained half-conscious for longer. As it was, the lord of Pemberwheeze's matrimonial day was not yet done, for he surfaced from an almost-swoon provoked by minor head trauma to find himself quite warm, being set near a crackling, albeit somewhat smoky, fire.

He was also held immobile, tied with stout hempen rope to a sturdy pillar holding up the thatched roof of what he recognized—with some faint consternation, through a throbbing headache—as a peasant domicile.

There was a splashing of something being stirred, and someone laughed nearby, a tinkling, silvery sound.

"But surely it can be done?" The laughing woman had a very aristocratic accent, and Byron felt he should know that voice. But his skull ached abominably, since he had landed upon it—perhaps an event of great misfortune, for it threatened to completely unmoor his wits.

Yet a lord of Chestthumper had to have a flinty pate indeed to conduct the business of Pemberwheeze, not to mention imbibe enough alcohol to cement his position in polite society, and Byron decided he was not quite dead or completely witless.

Yet.

"Not with the supplies I've on hand." The second female voice was faintly familiar as well, though her quivering accent was distinctly non-gentlewomanly. "Everyone thinks potions and simples are so easy. Well, if they were, plenty of other folk would be selling them instead of me."

The silvery-laughing woman's merriment had vanished, and she now became quite serious indeed. "How long?"

"A week." The older female let out a heavy sigh. "At least."

Byron's vision cleared a bit. He could see the fire, as well as a cluttered hearth, and smell something suspiciously like mutton stew as well as a reek of wet wool married to a sharp medicinal odor. There a blackened iron cauldron hung over the fire, and the steam from it boiled free, acting very strangely indeed. It fell instead of rising, and wreathed the orange flames with cottony yellow vapor.

"A *week*?" The gentlewoman did not think much of this. "But I've my Reputation to consider!"

"I've to go all the way to Pennyhampton for eye of newt. You think there's any newt left around here, what with Mrs Pingotts up the road mixing emetics and old Toadman Jekyll on the other side of the village needing roasted ones to keep him from his fits? And that's not even counting the tar I've to special order, to the rose-water to make it smell nice—"

Byron's eyes cleared even more. He stared about him, motionless and attempting to ascertain just what in blazes was going on.

"I suppose it won't help if I pay more?" A blonde woman, wrapped in a very dark cloak and with a veil distinctly askew, stood as if she rather feared something in the hut's interior would rub off on her fine fabric. "Double? Triple?"

"Oh, you could." The other woman, her graying hair scraped into a bun and her gown, sewn together from oddments and scraps, almost lost in a voluminous, tattered soldier's greatcoat, sniffed again, and spat into the fire, producing a brief crackle. "It won't make it come any faster, since the suppliers and distributors are all at sixes and sevens what with the pox running rampant and all, but I'll certainly appreciate your generosity."

The blonde lady absorbed this, and might have made

some manner of reply if the entire shack hadn't begun shuddering under a series of thunderous door-knocks.

"*Mother!*" a man yelled, muffled through said door. "*Mother, it's me, open up!*"

Byron blinked several times. He recognized at least one of the women, now that he'd had a bit of a chance to breathe.

But what on earth was Baroness Frostcunny doing *here*?

6

CHICKEN, DARLING

IT WAS QUITE AN EXCITING EVENING FOR CHICKEN, WHO disliked being taken from a warm stable to prance about the Heathencliffe Moors in a nasty thick fog. It took the pinkish mare some small while to realize her beloved two-legs—who Chicken considered not very bright but exceedingly loving, which covered many a fault—was no longer in the saddle.

She mightn't have discovered this for quite some while yet had not a very large black charger surrounded by a clot of baying hounds crossed her path at an angle instead of pursuing her, which caused Chicken to halt, digging her hooves in and throwing up clods of wet earth. The funny thing usually strapped to her forehead had slipped, quite irritating the mare, and she stood for a few moments, lathered and snorting, her tail flicking as she attempted to ascertain what her two-legs wanted in *this* ungodly situation.

But there was no weight upon her back, and were no knees pressing against her sides, and no soft, pretty hands upon her reins. Which, Chicken reasoned, meant that her two-legs had somehow vanished, and *that* was a concerning development.

After all, her two-legs knew just the right pressure to apply with a currycomb, and furthermore was never selfish with apple slices and other delicacies. Not to mention she told Chicken, over and over, that she was the most beautiful unicorn, a sentiment the mare did not quite grasp the complexity of but understood the affection within *quite* well.

Chicken listened as the black charger and his entourage cantered into the distance. Of course she could follow—where one horse went, another could go and be assured of at least some welcome, and besides, any horse liked the idea of a herd, even an almost-unicorn.

But the pinkish mare paused, for she was dimly aware her two-legs perhaps had not *intended* to vanish, which meant there was something very amiss indeed. A prey animal normally would react to this feeling with wild flight, but Chicken was rather worn out from all the excitement. Besides, the stable her two-legs had taken her from, while warm and comfortable, was certainly not the familiar environs of Velvette and thus, were suspect as anything new or strange must be.

Therefore, Chicken was in a state of deep equine thought, attempting to choose between several different imperatives and having little luck, when her pinkish ears perked and her very sharp horse-senses discerned something familiar.

It was a long shattering whistle riding the moors' night winds like a flying hag in some old two-leg stories, and Chicken knew that cry very well, for it was how her two-legs often called her from paddock or field. How her two-legs made the sound Chicken could not understand, for it was not a whinny nor a bugle, but those without hooves made all manner of strange sounds and it was not for a certain pinkish mare to discover why, only to avoid those noises which represented danger or discomfort and to follow those which meant the opposite.

Consequently, Chicken stamped one dainty hoof, listening intently. The thing on her forehead slipped frighteningly near her eyes, and she shook her head irritably, almost whipping the leather strap and short stuffed horn free.

The sound came again. It was definitely her two-legs, and she was calling her faithful steed. Which meant there was a prospect of returning to a stable, perhaps with a bucket or bag of mash, which was an outcome to this situation to be hoped for most devoutly. Better yet, it was *familiar*, and that meant safety. Once she had her two-legs firmly in the saddle where she belonged again, the world would be returned to its proper course.

The almost-unicorn turned further, head upflung, taut and ready. When the next whistle came, she set off at a determined trot, for it was indeed very dark and it would not do to put a hoof wrong.

Eventually, the silences between the whistles length-ened, and Chicken could tell her two-legs was becoming a wee bit fatigued. The mare scented water, a deep unhappy rotting-smell, and a thread of two-legs that were not hers. But she also caught a breath of Titness McHawttie's rose soap, and neighed.

"Oh good heavens," a familiar voice said, muffled but still clearly audible to a horse's sharp ears. "Finally."

Chicken found herself near a structure that was defi-nitely not a stable, for it smelled simply awful, lacking the homey tang of manure and other horses. She shook her head again, the stuffed horn bobbing embarrass-ingly. She bore with the thing because her two-legs evidently considered it necessary, but it was *irritating* and other horses sometimes mocked it.

Mockery was not to be borne, and Chicken generally attempted to bite those who engaged in the maneuver.

"Chicken?" her two-legs whispered. "Are you there?"

Chicken snorted. Apparently her two-legs was inside this tumbledown wooden cave, for whatever incompre-hensible reason. The mare flicked her tail again, faintly aware that this represented an obstacle to returning to a snug stall and a barrel of oats, not to mention a stable-boy or two to terrorize with her beady glare and strong teeth.

"Chicken, darling," her two-legs said, and rattled the door. "I hate to ask, but *perhaps* you could be of some use?"

Chicken cogitated upon this. She did not see what possible use she could be in this situation, and the entire affair was irritating beyond belief. Her two-legs belonged in the saddle, finishing whatever business had called them out in this dreadful chilly darkness, not inside some bloody shack.

"I don't suppose you have a key," her two-legs said, but horses have no concept of *keys* as such, only the sound of their jangle presaging food or work.

It occurred to Chicken that, amazingly, her two-legs was perhaps unable to perform the usual two-leg act of opening a door with clever little paws, and that it might, in fact, be up to a certain pinkish mare to solve the problem. The mare made a short, inquisitive sound, working this thought about in her equine brain.

"Oh, Chicken," her two-legs said from the other side of the door, "how I wish you could understand me, for—"

The almost-unicorn let out a shattering neigh, and reared. Her hooves battered the door, and the entire fish-shed shuddered. There was a yelp from inside, and Chicken landed heavily, cocking her head and waiting for some response.

"Good girl!" Titness McHawttie called, much more muffled since she was now observing a safer distance from the door. "Again, Chicken! Again! *Kick the bloody thing in, my faithful unicorn!*"

Now, the pinkish mare understood very few words, with the exceptions of *no, mash, apple,* and a few terms the stable-boys were wont to mutter as they mucked stalls. But her two-legs' tone of approbation—indeed, of outright delight—was extremely understandable, so Chicken decided to repeat the maneuver.

There was a great rending, tearing crash, a short scream from her two-legs.

Chicken reared again, and again.

7
EXCEPTIONS AND THIRTY THOUSAND

DUDLEY DEWBADDE LONGED TO RETURN TO THE PEACE AND quiet of Wystywych Lane, even though it was a cold foggy night and his fine Collective-owned trousers were slightly chafing since he had not worn them before and they were, while very flashy, also around a half-size too small. But he quite needed his mother's advice, as well as to look in on his home while waiting for the traffic about the Lane to clear, so to speak, and now he scratched at his temple, eyeing his dearest Mum, and attempted once more to make himself heard.

It was quite a difficult maneuver, since the man tied with stout hemp rope to the central pillar of the family hut—with knots, it must be said, much better than Dudley's own—was arguing rather vociferously with Ichabodia Dewbadde, and a stately blonde in a fine indigo cloak stood to one side, voicing a sardonic comment every once in a while which served only to apply fresh fuel to a conversational conflagration fast approaching a confrontation.

"I say, Mother, let the poor man—" Dudley halted, for the man tied to the pillar strained against his bonds again and the entire house creaked alarmingly.

"Untie me at *once!*" he roared. "I shall endure no more of this!"

"Oh, you look just like your father." Mother Dewbadde bent over, stirring the ever-fuming cauldron with a long, stained wooden spoon. "And I should know."

"There was no gossip at all," the tall, beautiful blonde woman said, and her violet eyes sparkled with mischief Dudley could barely look away from. "Are you *quite* certain, Mrs Dewbadde?"

"*You'd* remember it too if you rolled in the hay with Bysshe Blackheart." The widow smacked her lips, her grey eyebrows twitching. "Hung like a ruddy horse that man was, and knew how to use it."

"*Mother!*" Dudley gasped. He was quite used to Widow Dewbadde's less-than-polite references to certain of the neighbourhood gentry, but the blonde in the fine cloak was obviously a *lady*, and the decided tilt of her chin as well as the flash of her pretty eyes caused a strange sensation in his muscled chest.

"How dare you speak about my father like that!" The strange man strained against his bonds again, and the support pillar gave a deep, quite unnerving creak.

"Well, he was Dudley's father too," the widow

replied, sharply. "Now hush, lad, the adults are speaking. Thirty thousand, you say? And all yours?"

"Well, yes." The blonde lady clasped her gloved hands tightly, and her pert little nose wrinkled. Dudley quite longed to see her smile again. "I am the sole heir, you see, and the legal—oh, that doesn't matter. You see—"

"What in blazes do you want *him* for, then? Men are useless." The widow sighed, her wooden spoon splashing. "Oh, don't pull that face, Dudley, you know you're your sainted mother's exception to the rule. Come in and shut the door."

Belatedly, Dudley realized he was standing in the open aperture, letting all the heat out into a cotton-fogged, chilly autumn night. "Oh. Sorry, Mum."

"It's like I always say. Get 'em young, train 'em right." The widow nodded sagely.

"But it's my aunt de Bourguignon, you see." The blonde woman—oh, Dudley would have liked to see *her* in a fancy coach, she looked the type to have jewellery and her very large eyes caused him some exceedingly strange sensations—drew closer to the fire.

"She sounds like a soup," his mother said. "Made of beef, which I rather like, even though it gives one terrible gas."

"Hymenia." Apparently their prisoner recognized their golden-haired guest, for he now aimed his ire in her direction. "What the devil do you think you're doing?"

"It's your fault for marrying that McHawttie girl," she replied, tossing her pretty blonde curls in utterly bewitching fashion. "You know we were promised to each other from the cradle!"

"*I* never agreed to that," the prisoner snapped.

By now, Dudley rather thought he should have at least some grasp upon the situation, but he was even more puzzled than he had been when he opened the door and discovered the visitors—which was saying something. He had, truth be told, almost forgotten the redhead safely locked in the ramshackle fish-shed, and the inside of his skull was alive with quite an unwonted crumpling sensation as he attempted to suss out just precisely what he should do.

The feeling, though he did not know it since it was quite unfamiliar, was one which accompanied truly strenuous—instead of merely necessary—mental effort.

"Just a moment." Widow Dewbadde straightened as her son swept the door closed, which made the hut's sitting-room-slash-kitchen rather crowded indeed. "You still haven't answered the deeper question, Baroness."

A real, live baroness? In his mother's house? Of course some of the local worthies crept to the Dewbadde door at night for philtres and such—Dudley well remembered, as a sprout, gathering ditchwater and frog eggs, quite a few newts and an alarming amount of foxglove, not to mention nightshade, for his mother's concoctions. But it was the first time a *baroness* had appeared, especially one with purplish pansy eyes, slightly mussed corn-gold hair, and a fine bosom under her expensive navy wool cloak, not to mention a veil she irritably tucked aside with long, slim gloved fingers.

In short, Dudley was beginning to feel rather faint, but very glad he was dressed in the Sneak and Vicious Collective's best finery.

"You have thirty thousand pounds," Mother Dewbadde said, "and an estate. It's a pity about your neighbours, for the Blackhearts are a bad bunch—"

"Madam, I am not the one who has tied a complete stranger to a post, and plans to drug him," the visitor interrupted, and though Dudley did not like his tone, he had to admit the man had a point.

"He does have a point," Dudley said, rather faintly.

"*You* stay out of this," the baroness and his mother snapped in unison.

Dudley hunched his shoulders, looking—though he was rather handsome, being black of eye and hair like their guest, and sharing a certain breadth of chest and shoulder—very much like a turtle.

"I say," the man tied to the post said, studying Dudley closely. "You *do* look rather like my father, sir."

"My aunt de Bourguignon was *quite* vociferous upon the point more than once." The baroness spoke over him, addressing Widow Dewbadde. "The shades of Pemberwheeze Chase must not be polluted with some little northern hoyden—"

Dudley's mother's eyebrows nested in her greying hairline. "She said that?"

"No, she said that our estates used to be one and then the King—oh, *bother*, why am I giving a history lesson?" The blonde all but stamped one exquisitely dainty foot. "Just give him the tonic, and we shall be on our way."

"Now wait just a moment—" the bound man said.

"I told you it'll take at least a week." The widow gestured with her wooden spoon, and a bit of boiling mutton-broth splashed the prisoner, who let out a bellow and strained against his bonds yet again.

"I can't leave him here for a bloody *week*!" the baroness cried, and Dudley felt even more faint. She was positively enchanting, especially with high color in her cheeks and a vexed glint in her pansy eyes.

"No, you can't." The widow tested a bit of broth remaining on the spoon and nodded. "Maybe we should just kill him. Dudley, get your pistol."

"I already have it, Mum," he managed.

"By Jove, you can't really mean—" The prisoner was making a *lot* of noise.

"I don't want you to *kill* him." The baroness now *did* stamp her well-modeled foot, turned out nicely in a beautiful, expensive indigo leather riding boot. "I want you to give him a *love potion*."

"Poison, potion, what's the difference?" The widow sniffed, waving the spoon for emphasis again and narrowly avoiding splattering the bound man afresh. "Besides, if he's done for, my Dudley becomes the heir to Pemberwheeze Chase." Apparently this idea quite pleased Dudley's mother, for she gave a cackle and turned back to her stirring.

"Oh dear," Dudley said, thoughtfully. "I had not meant to *murder* tonight, only to hold up a coach or two."

The prisoner gave another mighty heave against the ropes, and the entire hut swayed upon its foundation.

8

ARSON, MURDER, SOUP

BAD ENOUGH THAT HE ACHED ALL OVER FROM A VERY embarrassing spill. But to be tied to a pillar and argued over in this fashion was far more than Byron Perssy Blackheart could stand, especially with a young man who looked very much like his late, unlamented father standing in the door of the prison-hut, which smelled of stew, medicine, a whiff of manure, and other things not nearly so nice.

All in all, his wedding day had turned out rather oddly, though he had to admit it was extremely exciting, and he suspected he would not be bored during the rest of his wedded existence. He gave one final heave against the beam he was tied to, and was rewarded with a great rending, splintering crash.

Several things happened at once.

Silly little Hymenia from next door let out a shriek like a fishmonger. Byron remembered her aunt de Bourguignon, a sour-faced old prude with fusty skirts and a habit of gripping the young Chestthumper's cheek with arthritic fingers while exhaling halitosis in his direction. In fact, it was quite fair to say that Baroness Frostcunny's plan of sending children to a very cold boarding school was her aunt's, for the old lady had raised her after the Galores had both died in that awful carriage accident. Instructed from a tender age by such a creature, no wonder Hymenia was behaving in such peculiar fashion.

But Byron's charitableness in his neighbour's direction was quite outweighed by his ire at being hobbled to a post like a horse—and where was Pickle, anyway? Byron was quite worried about his beloved black charger, and belatedly realized he should be worried for his new bride too. For while the high-spirited Titness had spat in his crumpets she had not attempted to tie him to furniture and furthermore was displaying a rather well-bred maidenly reticence to certain things marriage entailed, which meant at least she might not laugh at him for not quite knowing what to do in that area either.

At the same time, the young man who looked so dreadfully like his father was staring at Hymenia as if poleaxed, which would have been *quite* amusing had Byron simply been observing this entire event from the other side of a warm, well-lit drawing room.

Instead, he was in a stinking hut which shuddered one final time. Dust and thatching rained down, Hymenia shrieked afresh, the man who looked like Byron's father threw himself in her direction, and Widow Dewbadde began a round of cursing which *also* bore a distinct resemblance to Byron's late father, for Bysshe

Blackheart could fling obscenities with shocking alacrity when so moved.

And then the hut's roof—or at least, the portion over the sitting-room-slash-kitchen, but not the two small, rather snug bedrooms nor the privy 'round the back—caved in, and a great deal of thatching landed upon the fire.

As it had been a rather dry autumn until just now, the straw promptly caught fire, and Byron Blackheart found himself half-free of his bonds as a great quantity of smoke began to billow from the hearth.

"Oh, by *Christ's ass*," the beldam howled, "he's gone and ruined the soup!"

"Don't worry, my lady!" the young man who looked like Bysshe Blackheart cried loudly, at the very same moment. "Dudley of the Sneak and Vicious Collective will aid you!"

Hymenia did not precisely *say* anything; quite beyond words, she simply shrieked rather like a tea-kettle. Which reminded Lord Chestthumper of his new bride, who was out in the dark and quite possibly needed some manner of rescue if her night was proceeding anything like his own.

Consequently Byron Blackheart staggered upright, making his way through the thick smoke in the direction of the door. Or, more precisely, in the direction he reasoned the door must still be in, despite the state of the rest of the structure. More thatching fell, the wattle walls cracking, and a cold damp draught filtered in, giving the fire a great deal of breath.

The blaze took this invitation with cheerful readiness, making itself quite at home.

Byron tripped, rolled, and staggered back afoot with straw and dirt clinging to his hair, his coat, his breeches, and the rest of him as well. He found the latch and flung the door open, tripped once more over his own well-polished riding boots, and fell flat upon his face, attempting to catch himself upon his rather large hands and failing miserably.

This meant that when Widow Dewbadde was thrust from the interior by her loving son, still screaming bloody murder about her ruined mutton soup, she stamped upon Byron Blackheart's backside, his back proper, and his shoulder before hopping onto the beaten-dirt pathway leading to the Dewbadde cottage. "*Fire!*" she shrieked. "*Arson! Murder! Soup, oh, my beautiful soup! What a world, what a world!*"

Byron gathered what remained of his wits, and he might have also gained some approximation of an upright status if Dudley Dewbadde had not—rather heroically, it must be said—thrust Hymenia Galore through the door as well. The tall, shapely, and very frightened baroness stamped upon Byron's *other* buttock, then one of his kidneys, then his shoulder, and almost tripped as the toe of her indigo boot caught upon the back of his head. She staggered away, coughing from the smoke, and Byron once more attempted to rise.

There were no more heroics for Dudley to perform, so he quite prudently made his own escape through the door. It was a miracle he did not step upon his half-

brother's—for such was their relationship, apparently—
backside, but his own rather large highwayman's boot
landed between Byron's legs. Since Duds was moving
with all the speed he could muster, his other boot landed
somewhat beside Byron's hip, and the result of his
forward motion was his first foot's booted toe sinking
rather deep in the tenderest portion of Byron Blackheart's anatomy.

Lord Chestthumper gave a magnificent roar almost
twice as loud as the merrily burning blaze, which served
to alert the villagers of Snivvelings to danger but also
was cut off halfway as large, magnificently muscled
Dudley Dewbadde tripped and proceeded to fall flat
upon him.

9
THE EXCITEMENT OF SNIVVELINGS

THE EVENING MIGHT STILL HAVE REACHED A SATISFACTORY conclusion, Hymenia thought, if silly, stupid Byron had just cooperated, or if the beldam the baroness's old Nursie Givens had sworn was both effective and efficient proved to be either.

As it was, the Galore heiress found herself bellowing fire-fighting instructions in quite unladylike fashion, risking her cherished Reputation as a bucket brigade was set up from the mill-pond. The blazing cottage crackled and popped, Widow Dewbadde clutched Hymenia's arm while raving about her ruined soup, and Byron was dragged from the cottage door by the fellow who looked *alarmingly* like him, though rather handsomer and in ruffian-ish clothing, including a cutlass and a very fine feathered hat.

In short order the fire was extinguished—it was not the first time little Snivvelings Village had endured this kind of thing—and the commotion was just beginning to die down when a pinkish mare appeared, cantering along with a disheveled redhead clinging to her back. The redhead drew rein, regarding this scene with quite open surprise, and her pretty jaw nearly dropped when she recognized her new husband.

A soot-covered Lord Chestthumper, wincing as he moved, attempted to catch the mare's reins. "*Titness!*" he bellowed.

"Byron—" Hymenia whispered.

"My lady." Dudley Dewbadde, his hat somewhat cockeye and its feather draggled, attempted to sweep a bow in the baroness's direction. "I—"

"*My soup!*" the widow continued, at quite unladylike volume more fit for a battlefield than a quiet country village.

"Chicken!" The redheaded tart pulled on the reins, bringing the mare to a halt just short of Byron's clutching hands. The stuffed horn clinging to the beast's forehead was just as askew as Dudley's fetching, feathered hat.

"Titness!" Byron repeated, at somewhat lower volume.

"Byron..." the hussy who had stolen Pemberwheeze replied, breathlessly.

"Madam?" The rakish highwayman attempted once more to catch Hymenia's attention.

"Ichabodia!" Mr Rackham, the most eligible—though, it must be said, also most elderly—bachelor in the village hurried through the crowd, his old black silver-buckled hat barely clasped to his wig and his cane thumping.

"*My bloody soup!*" Widow Dewbadde yelled, then burst into tears not of sadness—for she had quite enough savings to rebuild her cottage in much sturdier fashion, and indeed had been thinking of burning the whole thing down herself—but of rage, for a good mutton soup was one of her very favorite things and had won ribbons at county fairs for seven years running.

"Oh, *Hell*," Hymenia said, freeing her arm from the beldam in quite decided fashion, turning upon one heel, and setting off for the inn, which was on the far end of the village from the moorside witch's hut and the picturesque mill-pond with its now sadly battered fish-shack.

"Wait a moment..." Caught between the urge to follow the statuesque blond goddess and the contradictory need to look after his mother, Dudley put a meaty arm over the widow's shoulders. "Oh, blast and botheration."

"Don't bother about *me*, Duds," his mother snapped, pointing after the baroness. "She's got thirty thousand pounds!"

"Oh, Byron." Titness, quite shocked, stared down at her new husband, quite forgetting she was vexed with him. "What on *earth* happened to you?"

"I, uh..." Lord Chestthumper was suddenly aware of the straw in his hair, the dirt clinging to his clothes, and the deep throbbing aches in several parts of his person, made all the worse by the distraction of Titness's capacious, heaving bosom and sparkling cornflower eyes. "I was, er, rather afraid you'd, um, be harmed, so I...I..."

"Are you hurt?" Mr Rackham said, coming to an arthritic stop nearby and whacking the dirt path with his cane for emphasis. "My dearest Ichabodia, shall I challenge one of these ruffians? Have you been harmed *in the slightest?*"

"Of course not, you dolt." The widow produced a large red-checked handkerchief from her sleeve, blew her sharp nose in decided fashion, and blinked at him. "But my soup is gone."

"You were worried?" Titness's forehead wrinkled quite charmingly, and her manner had thawed most prodigiously. She did hate to worry anyone, being at heart a rather kind creature. "Oh. I'm quite sorry about the crumpets, you see, I was just so—"

"Oh, I don't mind," Byron hastened to assure her, finally catching Chicken's reins. "But tell me, are you all right? You look rather upset, and if anything has happened to you I shall—"

"I was, er, locked in a shed..."

Hymenia left them all behind; a short walk returned her to the flea-bitten inn without further ado. The place was deserted, since there were exciting events afoot elsewhere in the village, and in short order Baroness Frostcunny was back in her verminous, very small room, where—with her Reputation all but ruined and her plans all gone awry—she could sob in peace.

IO

MATRIMONIAL HARMONY

So it was that Titness McHawttie was led back to Pemberwheeze Chase upon her faithful pinkish Chicken, a straw-covered and soot-tarnished Lord Chestthumper speaking very gently to the mare and to his new bride as well, and by the time they arrived—finding the whole estate in a bit of an uproar, for Pickle and the hounds had returned without their master—they had agreed that there was room *inside* the manor, not to mention the bedrooms, for no few of the Velvette pussies, and that the Pemberwheeze hounds could possibly be trained *not* to pursue the warm, furry things. Matrimonial harmony thus assured, everyone turned in for the night.

A very relieved Lord Chestthumper discovered his new bride had been thoroughly educated indeed by the finishing school at Lowe Crampton, and was quite capable of teaching him a few things. For her part, Titness discovered she did not mind her new husband as much as she thought, for he was willing to let his wife have her way in almost anything, and that, as every reasonable person knows, is the secret to most varieties of happy union.

In the morning, Hymenia Galore returned on foot to the vast Frostcunny estate, rather surprised—and, truth be told, a bit charmed—to be waylaid halfway there by a somewhat bedraggled highwayman of a certain Sneak and Vicious Collective, who found her even more breathtaking in daylight and quite forgot to utter the traditional *Stand and deliver*, instead stammering *Oh my goodness you're beautiful, even my mum says so*, which was just what the baroness needed to hear upon a day when she suspected her Reputation was gone for good.

Widow Dewbadde was fussed over at Mr Rackham's while her cottage was being rebuilt with no little aid from Lord Chestthumper, who had been heretofore unaware of his half-brother but was determined to settle a handsome living upon the lad until his advantageous marriage and a comfortable sinecure in perpetuity upon Dudley's mother, who he referred to ever after as "dear Aunt" and deferred to in all matters culinary.

Dudley and Hymenia were in fact married half a year later, with Byron as the best man and Titness as maid of honour, for they were, after all, neighbours. Titness even forgave Hymenia's habit of calling the lady of Pemberwheeze a tart, for she addressed the baroness as *my lady Hussy* in return, and so the two highly aristocratic beauties were something approaching amicable enemies for at least two years before they discovered they had quite a bit in common, not least the abject adoration of their husbands, and decided alliance was better than polite quasi-warfare.

It can also be said that Chicken and Pickle were caught several times in rather athletic sandwich-making while out at paddock or field, having no manners to keep such congress decently confined to the stable. Chicken's horn was lost during one of these encounters, and Titness moped a bit until a new one could be made.

And while all this proceeded the most eligible, even if elderly, bachelor of Snivvelings Village addressed himself to courtship of a certain Widow Dewbadde.

But that, my dear Reader, is another tale entirely...

THE END

AN ACKNOWLEDGING NOTE

This little romp had its genesis in a premade cover from my good friend Lady Skyla Dawn Cameron—an actual Lady, and with the paperwork to prove it. The premade is a real beauty and one day I shall write something "serious" for it, I promise.

It was the placeholder text that caught my eye, though. "She's Fleeing a Byronic Hero" made me think of those marvelous ol' gothic romances, young women with great hair running away from brooding mansions—and all of a sudden, the fires of inspiration flooded my soul, so I ran back to my workshop where, as Bette Midler would intone, I fussed and fussed and fussed.

The result is this story, whose tongue-in-cheek nature should not detract from the fact that it is, when all is said and done, a love song to a certain bundle of romance tropes.

Thanks are due not only to Skyla, who started the whole thing, but also to the faithful subscribers whose support allowed me the time to actually write it. Some are Tuckerized, others provided hilarious references, and the number of in-jokes, not to mention callbacks (in the best Rocky Horror tradition), approaches near-insanity.

I hope this small tale provides a chuckle, and a gentle tweak under the skirt of convention. And now I shall cease my blathering (not that anyone ever reads these notes anyway, except certain completionists like yours truly) and go about my business...

...which is to thank my beloved Readers in the way we both like best, by telling yet another tale.

See you around.

About the Author

Her Ladyship Alana Smithee is a pseudonym, and very glad of it.

Printed in Great Britain
by Amazon

79892038R00038